Jeffrey and the Fourth-Grade Ghost

Max Is Back

Other
Jeffrey and the Fourth-Grade Ghost
Books

#2 Baseball Card Fever
#3 Max's Secret Formula

And
Jeffrey and the Third-Grade Ghost

#1 Mysterious Max
#2 Haunted Halloween
#3 Christmas Visitors
#4 Pet Day Surprise
#5 Max Onstage
#6 Max Saves the Day

Jeffrey and the Fourth-Grade Ghost

BOOK ONE

Max Is Back

Megan Stine
AND
H. William Stine

FAWCETT COLUMBINE
NEW YORK

To Aunt Bess—
Better late than never,
in both book dedications
and relationships.

—H. W. S.

Recommended for grades two to four

A Fawcett Columbine Book
Published by Ballantine Books
Copyright © 1989 by Cloverdale Press, Inc.

Library of Congress Catalog Card Number: 89-91679

ISBN: 0-449-90415-6

Text design by Mary A. Wirth
Illustrations by Marcy Ramsey

Manufactured in the United States of America
First Edition: September 1989
10 9 8 7 6 5 4 3 2 1

Chapter One

"Get out of the way! Look ouuut!" Jeffrey Becker shouted at the top of his lungs.

Too late. Jeffrey had time to shout his warning, but the man on the sidewalk didn't have time to jump out of the way. Jeffrey and his skateboard zoomed right into the puddle in front of the man. And the man was the principal of the school!

One minute Mr. Dunwoodie was smiling and greeting students on the first day of school. The next minute Mr. Dunwoodie was splattered with puddle water.

"Not wasting any time this year, are you, Jeffrey?" mumbled the principal as he brushed at his jacket, trying to dry off.

"I'm sorry, Mr. Dunwoodie. I'm really sorry," Jeffrey apologized.

But the principal didn't stop frowning. "Jeffrey, are you trying to get a detention *before* the school year even begins? I think that's a new school record. Why didn't you watch where you were going?"

"I'm totally sorry, Mr. Dunwoodie," Jeffrey said quickly. "It wasn't my fault. It was . . ."

Jeffrey's voice trailed off. Should he tell the truth? Or should he do what he always did in situations like this: make up a fantastic and funny story? He thought about it for a minute and decided to go with the story—because there was no way Mr. Dunwoodie would believe the truth.

"Well?" Mr. Dunwoodie asked. "I'm waiting for your explanation, Jeffrey."

"Uh, yeah," Jeffrey said, thinking quickly. "Well, you see, Mr. Dunwoodie, it was the squirrel."

"The squirrel, Jeffrey?"

"Uh, yes, the squirrel that was walking across the sidewalk. It was a cute little baby squirrel."

Mr. Dunwoodie was known to be a softy when it came to anything furry. He smiled.

"That's how it all happened," Jeffrey went on. "I was skateboarding to school when suddenly a squirrel ran out in front of me. In fact, it was a whole family of squirrels—with three little babies. They all walked right in front of me as I was coming down the sidewalk. I had to swerve to miss them. I think I saved their lives. But unfortunately, Mr. D."—Jeffrey did his best to look upset—"I splashed you."

The principal nodded. "Jeffrey, you know what I want you to do now?"

"Go to the office and wait for you, just like I did last year?" Jeffrey guessed.

"No," the principal said, shaking his head. "I want you to be very proud of yourself. You're thinking and acting like a fourth-grader—and telling the truth. No more stories and no more detentions. This isn't going to be like last year, is it, Jeffrey?"

"No way, Mr. D.," said Jeffrey. "Nothing like last year."

As soon as the principal walked away, Jeffrey let out a long sigh of relief. That was a close one, he thought. He hated to start off the year with a lie, but how could he tell the principal the truth? How could he say: "The reason I ran into you is because I have a friend who is a ghost. His name is Max and he was skateboarding behind me—although he doesn't need a skateboard because he can fly. And when we got to the puddle, Max gave me a giant shove. He wasn't trying to get you wet,

Mr. Dunwoodie, just me. Max thinks things like that are cool."

It just wouldn't work.

"Hey, Max! Where are you?" Jeffrey called. "Do you know what I could have gotten for a hit-and-run on the principal?"

"Like, probably a detention, Daddy-o," said a voice near Jeffrey's ear.

As Jeffrey grinned, the ghost began to materialize. He was fading in and out and coming into focus like a television set being turned on. Max was about Jeffrey's age and Jeffrey's size, but he didn't look like any other kid in Jeffrey's class—because Max was from the 1950s. Max was combing his greased hair straight back and being careful not to disturb the curl that dipped over the middle of his forehead.

"You gotta be cool, Daddy-o, or you're from squaresville," said the ghost, stuffing the comb into the back pocket of his baggy blue jeans with the rolled cuffs. He looked at the school building and shook his head. "First day of school. Like, this must be about the hundredth time I've done this scene."

Jeffrey squinted one eye at his friend. "You're not that old," he said, knowing that Max was as big a storyteller as he was. That

4

was one reason why they liked each other so much.

Just then a loud bell rang. Jeffrey was late for class on the first day of school. "Max, let's go. I'm late. Hurry up." He started to run up the stairs to the front door, but the ghost grabbed his arm and held it.

"Jeffrey, like, cool it with the hurrying. Have you ever dug the fact that some of the world's most uncool words rhyme with hurry? Scurry, flurry, Murray, and jury, to lay a few of them on your ears."

"Jury?" Jeffrey echoed in disbelief. "Max, quit stalling. Let's get inside. This is the first day of school, and you know what that means, don't you?" He grinned. "A new teacher to drive crazy. And a few days when we can get away with anything. Besides that, we're fourth-graders now."

"What do you mean 'we'?" the ghost asked, shaking his head. "Daddy-o, like, I was in the third grade right before I took my one-way trip to ghostsville, and I've been there ever since. Of course, I could have gone into the fourth grade any time I wanted. But, like, who wants to? If fourth grade is so cool, then why do cats only stay there *one year*?"

"People only stay in third grade one year, too," Jeffrey replied. "At least most of them do." He cocked his head a little to the side and brushed his thick brown hair out of his eyes so that he could see his friend better. "Max, are you scared to go into the fourth grade or something?"

"Like, nothing scares a ghost," Max told him, crossing his arms in front of his chest.

"Well, then, let's go," Jeffrey said. He ran up the stairs. But when he turned around at the front door to make sure that Max was coming, Max had disappeared.

He'll sneak into class, Jeffrey told himself. He'll be there, waiting to surprise me. No way is that ghost just going to stay in third grade.

But when Jeffrey walked into his new fourth-grade classroom, Max was not there. Class had not begun yet, so Jeffrey quickly slipped into the seat that was being saved for him—right between his best friend, Benjamin Hyde, and his next-door neighbor, Melissa McKane. Ben and Melissa, along with Kenny Thompsen and Ricky Reyes, were Jeffrey's good friends. They were also the only people besides Jeffrey who could see Max.

"Has she said anything yet?" Jeffrey asked, motioning toward their new teacher.

"No," Ben said. He was consulting the stopwatch mode of his watch. "According to my calculations, I predict she won't say anything for exactly sixty-three seconds."

"What do you think Miss Dotson will say?" asked Melissa, tucking her long red ponytail up under her baseball cap.

"I don't know," Jeffrey answered. "But listen carefully to her first words. It's the key to everything."

According to Jeffrey's theory, the first words a teacher said on the first day of school predicted exactly what kind of year it was going to be.

If the teacher said "Good morning," it would be a friendly and fun year.

If the teacher immediately started to call the roll from the roll book, it was going to be a follow-the-rules kind of year.

And if the first thing the teacher said was "Your homework for tomorrow is . . ." that was M.T.: Major Trouble.

The final bell rang. The school year had officially begun.

"Okay, you guys. This is it," Jeffrey said.

One by one the students stopped talking and waited to hear their teacher's first words.

The teacher was a white-haired, elderly woman—in fact, she was the oldest teacher at Redwood Elementary School. Her name was Miss Dotson. She stood in front of the class wearing a dark blue dress with small white polka dots. Finally she cleared her throat and took a deep breath. "Merry Christmas and have a good winter vacation," she announced in her loud but gravelly voice.

Merry Christmas? Those were her first words? Buckle your seatbelts, Jeffrey told himself. This was going to be a totally *weird* year!

"Miss Dotson," Becky Singer called out, raising her hand after she had already spoken. Becky was Melissa's best friend. And she was usually the first person to point out a mistake—especially a teacher's mistake. "Today is the first day of school, Miss Dotson, not the last day before vacation."

"Oh, that's right. I forgot," Miss Dotson said, nodding in agreement. "And the first thing we should do is introduce ourselves. Let's start with you."

8

So Becky Singer started and they went around the room. One by one the kids told Miss Dotson their names. But even though Miss Dotson listened carefully, and even though she had a list of everyone in the class, she couldn't seem to remember a single name! She called Arvin Pubbler "Marvin." She confused Jenny Arthur with Kenny Thompsen, which made Kenny's face turn red because he was very shy. Kenny knew everyone in the cafeteria would tease him and call him Jenny for weeks. She called Jeffrey "Jerry." And for some reason, she kept calling Melissa "Gertrude."

Max would love this, Jeffrey thought. He'd get a real jolt out of Miss Dotson. So why hadn't he come to class? Jeffrey looked around the room expectantly.

After the roll was checked, Miss Dotson started looking around her desk for her assignment book. "What did I do with it?" the forgetful teacher muttered. The class watched as she picked up every item on her desk, searching for the assignment book.

This could be good, Jeffrey thought. If she doesn't find it, maybe we won't get any assignments.

9

But after a few minutes Miss Dotson found her assignment book and classwork began in earnest. Jeffrey realized with surprise that even though Miss Dotson was absentminded, she knew a lot about history, math, and geography. And even though she was not so good at remembering kids' names, she was very good at remembering to give homework. By lunchtime Jeffrey and his classmates had four assignments that were due that week.

School didn't get any better in the afternoon. Max was still missing—and Miss Dotson gave a first-day-of-class spelling quiz.

The test was almost over when Melissa turned around and whispered to Jeffrey, "How do you spell 'sensational'?"

"That's not one of the spelling words," Jeffrey whispered back.

"I know," Melissa said. "I finished the quiz. I'm writing in my diary."

Before Jeffrey could answer, Miss Dotson's voice pierced the air. "Just hold on a minute, Gertrude," she said, looking right at Melissa and then walking straight toward her. Melissa tried to put her diary away quickly, but she wasn't quick enough. Miss Dotson picked it up. "What are you doing, Gertrude?"

"I'm finished with my test," Melissa said. "Honest."

"I can see that, dear," Miss Dotson told her. "But I'll just put this away where you won't be tempted to write in it during class time." She carried the diary to her desk and dropped it into a desk drawer.

"Oh, no," Melissa moaned. Then she turned around and looked at Jeffrey. "Where's Max?" she asked.

Jeffrey shrugged. "That's what I was wondering, too."

"Well, get him," Melissa said. "I need him now!"

Chapter Two

After school Jeffrey's friends all crowded around him on the school's front lawn.

"Jeffrey, we've got to talk," Melissa said. "This teacher is the worst! Do you believe she called me Gertrude all day? And then she rushed off to a teachers' meeting without even giving my diary back!"

"We've got to talk, all right," Kenny agreed. "I am *not* going to go through the whole year being called by a girl's name. It's humiliating."

"Chill out, Kenny," Jeffrey said. "Maybe Miss Dotson is only calling us by the wrong names to get our attention. And no one else has called you Jenny."

"Hi, Jenny," Ben called as he joined the group.

"Not funny," Kenny said, fuming.

"I wasn't talking to you," Ben told him. "I was talking to *her*."

Kenny turned around and saw Jenny Arthur passing behind him.

"Great. Now I'm even answering to a girl's name!" Kenny muttered, his face turning red. "Jeffrey, we've got to do something—and fast!"

"I totally agree," Jeffrey said. "But what?"

"We need Max," Kenny and Melissa both said at once. "Why didn't he come to school?"

"I think he's afraid of the fourth grade . . ." Jeffrey started to explain. But before he could say anything more, a car horn blasted.

Jeffrey looked around and saw his mother's car parked at the curb. "What's she doing here?" he wondered out loud as he walked to the car.

His mother greeted him with a smile. "Hey, sparky, how'd it go?" she asked in a cheery voice.

"Great, Mom, just great. We have a totally weird teacher. You never know when she's going to be nice, when she's going to give us really hard work, or when she's going to be off-the-wall bonkers." Jeffrey looked at his mother suspiciously. "Couldn't you wait till I got home to find out? You know I always walk home with my friends."

13

"Get in," Mrs. Becker said. "I've got a terrific surprise for you. I've signed you up for an after-school pottery class."

"No thanks, Mom," Jeffrey said quickly. "I don't want an after-school activity. I want to be with my friends. We were just about to have a very important discussion about, uh, the meaning of life."

"The meaning of life can wait, sweetie," said his mother. "Pottery class starts in ten minutes."

"You mean today?" Jeffrey sputtered. "I'm going into another classroom *today*? Mom, I'm a kid. I need fresh air and exercise."

"You need to feel the earth in your hands," said Mrs. Becker.

"Okay, I'll roll around on the ground all afternoon," Jeffrey replied. "I promise."

"Pottery class. Eight minutes. Get in the car—now," Mrs. Becker said calmly.

Jeffrey climbed into the car. He had lost count of how many times the word *now* was the last word in an argument with his mom.

He waved to his friends as his mother drove away.

When they arrived at the YMCA, Mrs.

14

Becker smiled. "Your father and I think it's very important for you to get involved in a lot of different experiences," she told him "Especially this year."

"Why this year?" Jeffrey asked.

"Oh, certain reasons," she said with another mysterious smile. "You'd better hurry or you'll be late."

Jeffrey didn't care at all about being late. All he wanted was to be with his friends and to be with Max. Instead he was with ten strange kids. They were sitting on small chairs around a large table in a windowless basement classroom. In front of everyone was a mound of soft, wet clay about the size of a football.

"Now, class," said the instructor, a young man named Carl. He walked around the room, constantly squeezing a lump of clay in his hands. "There are several techniques for making beautiful clay objects. Today we will be starting with something easy, a basic candy dish or an ashtray."

"No sweat, Daddy-o," said Max's voice in Jeffrey's ear. "Arts and crafts are my specialty."

15

"They are?" Jeffrey asked.

"What are?" Carl asked him without a smile.

"Nothing," Jeffrey mumbled.

"I see," Carl said. "And next week," he continued, "we'll learn how to do what potters call 'throwing pots.'"

"Daddy-o, like, I'm already a natural at that," Max said to Jeffrey. As soon as he said it, one small red pot lifted off a table and flew against a wall, smashing into pieces.

No one saw Max throw the pot, but everyone saw the pot sail across the room.

"How could that have possibly happened?" asked the stunned teacher.

"Maybe you put it together with airplane glue," said Jeffrey, trying to hide a smile.

Pottery class was more fun than Jeffrey expected, thanks to Max. The ghost liked to make ashtrays, and made them very quickly. By the end of class Jeffrey had fifteen ashtrays sitting on his desk. Carl told him he was remarkable. But when Jeffrey turned to wink at Max, he realized that the ghost had vanished.

Max didn't appear again that day. He didn't ride home with Jeffrey and Mrs. Becker or show up in Jeffrey's room that night. There

16

was no chance to talk to him about joining the fourth grade.

The next day Jeffrey, Ricky, Ben, and Kenny walked to school together, hoping to see the ghost. But Max didn't show up and neither did Melissa. She had left for school early so that she could talk with Miss Dotson. Jeffrey and his friends walked into the class-room just in time to hear their conversation.

"Miss Dotson, may I have my diary?" Melissa was saying to the teacher.

"Yes, I think everyone should have a diary," said the teacher. "But you should ask your parents to give you one, Gertrude, not me."

"Miss Dotson," Melissa said, trying to re-main calm, "*you* have my diary. You took it yesterday and put it in your desk, and you never gave it back."

The teacher was resting her chin in her hands and listening hard to what Melissa was saying. She looked totally caught up in the story. "And then what happened?" Miss Dot-son asked.

"And then I didn't get it back," Melissa said.

Miss Dotson shook her head, as if this were the first time she'd heard of Melissa's diary. "Well," she replied, "I'll have to give it back to you when school is over today."

Melissa sighed with relief. "Great," she said. "Okay. As long as I get it after school."

But after school things didn't go much better. Miss Dotson dismissed the class without saying anything about Melissa's diary. So Melissa hung around until all of the kids had left the room. Jeffrey waited with her. Then they went up to Miss Dotson's desk.

"Miss Dotson, may I have my diary now?" Melissa asked.

"What diary, dear?" the teacher said pleasantly. "Do you have a diary?"

"Jeffrey, what am I going to do now?" Melissa whispered.

"Try offering her money," Jeffrey suggested.

"He's a kidder, isn't he?" Miss Dotson said with a wink at Melissa.

"I want my diary, Miss Dotson," said Melissa.

"Well, of course you do. What happened to it?" asked the teacher. "Did you lose it?"

Jeffrey could see that Melissa's patience was growing as thin as a single strand of her red hair.

"No," Melissa said slowly. "I didn't lose it. You took it from me. Don't you remember?"

"Of course I remember that," the teacher said. "But I gave it back to you this morning."

Melissa stamped her foot. "No, you didn't. You kept it. It's in your drawer." She turned to her friend. "Jeffrey Becker, will you help me?"

"Uh, well, you see, Miss Dotson," Jeffrey began, talking even faster than ideas were coming to him, "that diary is very important to Melissa because, uh, because there's something very important in it."

"Sounds interesting," said the teacher. "What is it?"

"A list," Jeffrey answered. "A very important list of, uh, every baseball signal ever used by Tommy Lasorda. Yeah, that's it. Our baseball team would be lost without Melissa's diary."

"Boy!" exclaimed Miss Dotson, standing up excitedly. "He can tell 'em, can't he?" She gave Melissa another wink.

"Please look in your drawer, Miss Dotson," pleaded Melissa.

"My pleasure," said the elderly woman, pulling open her desk drawer.

Jeffrey and Melissa moved in closer and stared down into it in surprise. The drawer was crammed full of things: pencils and papers and newspaper clippings and notebooks and flashcards and road maps and recipes and a sun hat and dark blue tennis shoes and a coffee cup and a can opener and diagrams of animal skeletons—and that was just the top layer.

"Face it, Melissa," Jeffrey said. "If your diary *was* in there, something probably already ate it."

Melissa ran out of the room and Jeffrey followed her.

"This is all your fault, Jeffrey," Melissa said, when Jeffrey finally caught up with her in the hall. "I told you we needed Max. I told you Max could help me."

"Then it's Max's fault," Jeffrey said reasonably.

"Well, Max isn't here, but you are. So I'm blaming you."

"Hey, Daddy-os!" Max suddenly began to appear. And in just a few seconds he looked as real as Melissa and Jeffrey—although no one else could see him. Max leaned against a locker. "Like, where did you cats learn to fight like that? In the big grade number four?"

"Max! Where have you been?" Melissa asked. "You've got to help me."

"Like, I thought fourth-graders knew how to do everything," said the ghost.

"Everything except convince a certain ghost I know to come to the fourth grade," Jeffrey said, staring hard at Max.

"What for?" asked Max. "Like, I heard the teacher is so flakey, she lives in a cereal bowl."

"What? Miss Dotson? You'd love Miss Dotson," Jeffrey said. "We do, *don't we*, Melissa?"

"Sure," Melissa said, but she almost choked on the word.

"She never gives us any work. She just tells jokes all day," Jeffrey lied.

"Yeah, like, I know about teachers' jokes. They're so oldsville they're rusty," said the ghost. But he was waiting anxiously to hear what Jeffrey would say next.

"No way," argued Jeffrey. "New jokes. Jokes you've never heard before. And you know what happened today?"

"What?"

Jeffrey suddenly realized that he didn't know what to say next. "Uh, tell him, Melissa," Jeffrey said.

"I can't," Melissa said with a blank look.

"Come on, Daddy-os. Lay it on me. Like, I can take it."

"Uh, it was a party, Max," Jeffrey said. "Miss Dotson baked a cake for Arvin Pubbler—and it wasn't even his birthday! She said she just felt like having a party. I'm telling you, Max. It's like that every day."

"Don't you want to come to class with us, Max?" Melissa asked.

"Like, maybe," said the ghost. Then he disappeared quickly, as if someone had pulled his plug.

"Do you think your story worked?" Melissa asked when Max was gone.

"Like, maybe," Jeffrey said.

Chapter Three

But for the next two days nothing changed. Max didn't come to class. Melissa didn't get her diary back. And Miss Dotson didn't stop calling people by the wrong names.

To make matters worse, Jeffrey didn't have time to go looking for Max. Every day after school his mother was waiting for him in the car. She had signed him up for more after-school activities.

On Tuesday it was Cooking for Boys. Jeffrey almost gagged when they made Stewed Tomato Cake. On Wednesday it was karate, which would have been cool, but at the first class the instructor passed out a huge textbook. "We're going to start by reading the history of Japan," he announced.

And worst of all, Max didn't even show up at night in Jeffrey's room. Max was, as Max would say, gonesville.

Or was he? Maybe he was hanging around invisibly, watching and listening to everything Jeffrey did and said. Jeffrey decided to set a trap for him—with Ben's help. On Wednesday night Ben came over to Jeffrey's house to do homework. After they finished their math, they sat in Jeffrey's room, talking.

"So what are you going to wear to the party tomorrow?" Jeffrey asked Ben.

"Oh, you mean the funny-nose party at *school*?" Ben said loudly. "Well, I've invented an electronic nose that blinks red and blue and makes sniffling noises." Ben was a whiz at science. He wanted to be an inventor when he grew up. "How about you, Jeffrey?"

Jeffrey reached into his drawer and pulled out a stubby, pink pig's nose. He put it on and looked at himself in the mirror. "This one," he said. "Too bad Max won't be there. He'd be a riot during Funny Nose Day."

Suddenly, another face appeared in Jeffrey's mirror. The trap had worked! It was Max.

"As the ice cream said to the milk, what's shaking, Daddy-os?" said the ghost with a grin.

"Hi, Max," Jeffrey said. "Notice anything

25

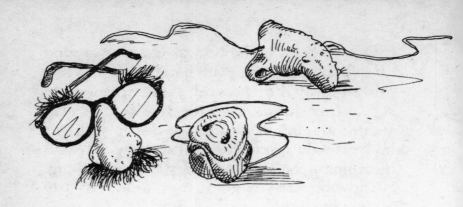

different?" He twitched the rubber nose on his face.

"No," Max teased, pretending not to notice the nose. "But did I hear the word 'party'?"

"Yeah," Jeffrey said. "In the *fourth* grade we do cool things like having Funny Nose Day at school. Don't you want to come?"

"Daddy-o, yours truly thought of Funny Nose Day, like, when I was in the second grade," said the ghost. "It was almost declared a national holiday."

"Why almost?" asked Ben.

"Because no one could hear what I was saying when I was wearing my nose. I told them the holiday was supposed to be called Funny Nose Day, but those cats thought I said Valentine's Day, so that's what they named it."

Ben laughed, and the ghost moved over to

Jeffrey's bed. He flipped through the pages of a magazine pretending to read it. But Jeffrey knew Max was only pretending, because it was a magazine about real estate. Jeffrey's mom had left it there by mistake.

"You know, Daddy-o, like, I've been thinking about school."

"Yeah? How's third grade, Max?" Jeffrey asked. He sat down backward on his desk chair and faced the ghost.

"It's a gas, Daddy-o, just like the year before and the year before and the year before that," the ghost said.

"Yeah, but *we're* not there," said Ben. "Don't you want to come to the fourth grade and be with us?"

"Come on, cats. You know my motto: If it isn't cool, it isn't Max. And fourth grade isn't cool."

"It could be," Jeffrey said.

Max looked at Jeffrey and Ben for a minute.

"You know what my ears are digging?" Max asked. "I'm beginning to groove that you cats miss me. That this ghost is the life of the party. That you cats are so *for*lorn, you're five-lorn without yours truly."

"Yeah, I guess we are," Jeffrey said sadly.

27

"It's not the same without you."

"Well, like, why didn't you say so?" asked the ghost.

"You mean, you'll come to class?" asked Ben.

"Not every day," said the ghost, "but, like, I might make the scene for a little visit."

Max waited until late the next afternoon to "visit" Miss Dotson's classroom. Jeffrey couldn't see him, but he knew the ghost was there the minute Arvin Pubbler started sneezing. Arvin liked to put his head down during class, and "someone" had sprinkled a little pepper on his desk.

A moment later Miss Dotson unrolled a long banner with large, glittery letters. It said: PHOTOSYNTHESIS. "Okay, class," she began, "can anyone tell me what this word is?"

"Like, it must be the runner-up in the longest-word-in-the-world contest," Max said.

Jeffrey, Melissa, Ricky, Kenny, and Ben grinned at each other. Max was back! But since no one else heard him, the other kids just looked at Jeffrey and his friends strangely.

"Who can tell me something important about photosynthesis?" the teacher asked. "Give it a try, Jerry!"

It took Jeffrey a moment to realize that she meant him. "Uh, gee, Miss Dotson, the truth is I'm not allowed to know," he said, thinking quickly. "I've asked my parents probably a hundred times to tell me what photosynthesis is, and they always say the same thing. 'You're not old enough.' So if you're going to talk about it, I'd better leave the room."

Miss Dotson frowned. "Well, obviously Jerry doesn't know, so I'll give the rest of you a hint: Photosynthesis is a combination of two words. What are they?" she asked, pointing behind her to the chalkboard.

But when Jeffrey looked at the board, he laughed. So did everyone else in the room. Written on the board was BE COOL.

Miss Dotson erased the words with her sleeve. "How did that get there?" she wondered aloud.

Jeffrey didn't have to wonder for a minute. He knew it was Max! Max was just getting used to the new classroom. Now this was what school was supposed to be like!

"What was I talking about?" Miss Dotson asked.

"Lunch," said Arvin Pubbler, trying to change the subject.

29

"Yes, lunch. Thank you, Marvin. And lunch reminds me of photosynthesis. Now, does anyone know what it is?"

"I don't know, but, like, I'm not cleaning it up," Max said to his friends. Jeffrey and Ben laughed. Max could get away with anything!

While Miss Dotson was writing on the board again, Max suddenly appeared. He was sitting in the empty seat in front of Becky Singer. "Hey, Daddy-o," Max called, waving to Jeffrey, "your teacher-o takes the cake."

Suddenly, Miss Dotson turned around. "Who said that?" she demanded. Her head jerked toward Max. "What are *you* doing in my classroom?" she asked.

To everyone else, it looked as if Miss Dotson was talking to Becky Singer. But to Jeffrey it almost looked as though the teacher was staring at the ghost. "Who are you?" Miss Dotson asked.

"Me?" Becky shrieked.

"No, you!"

Jeffrey couldn't believe it. She *was* looking and pointing straight at Max!

"Come on. Speak up. I want some answers," Miss Dotson said.

Jeffrey's heart almost stopped. And Max's eyes were about as big as his wide-open mouth. For once, both Max and Jeffrey were speechless! Finally Max tried to put the cool expression back on his face. "Like, you mean you can see me?" he stammered.

"Of course I can see you," the white-haired teacher said with a smile. "And I'm trying to find out why you are in my classroom. You aren't on my class list."

"Like, I'm not in the phone book, either," said Max.

"I don't believe this," Ben whispered to Jeffrey.

"Who's she talking to?" Brian Carr asked. Most of the class giggled. They thought Miss Dotson was just acting crazy. It looked as if she was having a conversation with someone invisible.

But Jeffrey and his friends stared at each other for a different reason. Unbelievable as it was, their teacher could see and talk to Max!

"All right. I won't take up valuable class time right now," Miss Dotson said to Max. "See me after class and I'll give you a copy of the homework."

"Look, teacher-o," said Max, "like, this scene is wigging me out. *You* can't give me homework."

"And why not?" asked Miss Dotson.

"Teacher-o, hold on to your chalk, but, like, yours truly doesn't do homework. Yours truly is a ghost."

Miss Dotson didn't say anything at first. She looked at Max, at his old-fashioned hair and clothes. Then she noticed that she could see through his legs. "You know, I thought so," she finally said with a confident shake of her head. "Well, I don't care if you're a strawberry shortcake. If you're in my class, you do your homework."

"Then forget your class and forget you," Max said angrily, standing up. He pushed against his desk as he stood, and it fell over onto its side.

Everyone stared at the desk, which looked as if it had fallen over by itself.

"You just earned yourself a detention for that," Miss Dotson told Max.

"A detention? I didn't do anything!" shrieked Becky Singer, who still thought Miss Dotson was scolding her.

"Like, you'll never see *me* in detention,"

Max said as he floated toward the door. "Because—dig this—you'll never see me in this squaresville school again!"

Max slammed the door on his way out. Then he was gone.

Chapter Four

One week later Jeffrey was asleep in his bed, dreaming. And in his dream everything was different, everything was okay. In the dream Max hadn't been gone for a whole week. In the dream Melissa hadn't lost her diary. And in the dream Jeffrey hadn't been to a different after-school program every day. It was wonderful . . . but it was only a dream.

"Jeffrey . . . Jeffrey."

It was his father's voice. What was he doing in the dream?

"Jeffrey, it's time to wake up," said Mr. Becker, sitting on the edge of Jeffrey's bed. He shook Jeffrey's shoulder gently.

Jeffrey opened his eyes. "Oh, yeah," he said, sort of smiling. "Where's Mom?"

"Not feeling perfect. Get dressed. I'll throw breakfast in the microwave."

"Forget it, Dad," Jeffrey called as his father

34

left the room. "The last time you made corn flakes in the microwave, it was a real mess."

Jeffrey got out of bed. I was dreaming, he thought. Back to reality. Max was still gone.

Then Jeffrey noticed the time: six-thirty. He got dressed sleepily, then went looking for his father.

"Dad," Jeffrey said, going into the kitchen, "I wanted to get up for school, not for the sunrise. Why did you wake me up so early?"

"It's Friday," Mr. Becker told him.

For a minute Jeffrey thought his father was giving him another one of those parents' reasons. They were reasons that always made complete sense to adults but never to kids.

"Dad, I know it's Friday. But what's that got to do with getting me up at six-thirty?"

"Jeffrey," said Mr. Becker between bites of an English muffin, "don't you remember? Early Morning School Band starts today."

Band! Of course! This wasn't one of those horrible after-school classes his mom had enrolled him in. This was something Jeffrey himself had signed up for. In fact, he had done it a long time ago—during the summer. He had always wanted to play the drums. This was going to be his chance at last.

"I forgot," Jeffrey said, drumming the table with his cereal spoon. "This is great!"

"Well, your mom and I knew how much you wanted to be in the band. And I've got a surprise for you."

Mr. Becker lifted something from his lap and slid it across the breakfast table toward Jeffrey. It was a small, hard, rectangular, leather-bound case. It had locks that snapped open at the push of a button.

"What is it?" Jeffrey asked suspiciously.

"Can't go to band without an instrument," Mr. Becker said.

Jeffrey opened up the case and found the four disassembled pieces of a black clarinet. "You've got to be kidding," he said, totally horrified.

"A couple lessons, and you'll be a rock 'n' roll superstar." Mr. Becker smiled at Jeffrey.

"Dad, do you know exactly how many rock 'n' roll clarinet players there are?"

"I guess I lost count," said Mr. Becker.

"Negative three," Jeffrey told him. "I told you months ago, Dad, I want to play the *drums*!"

"Jeffrey, when I was in school, *I* played that very same clarinet."

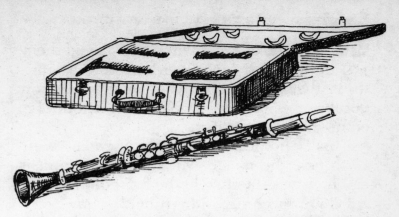

"But, Dad," Jeffrey argued, "aren't you the person who always said you hoped I wouldn't make all the same mistakes you did?"

Mr. Becker laughed. "Jeffrey, you've got to try all kinds of things to find out where you really belong."

"Sure, Dad, sure. That's great advice. I'm writing it down on my napkin right now. But do I have to play the clarinet?"

"Only for seventeen years," answered Mr. Becker. "Then if you don't like it, you can quit."

After breakfast Mr. Becker drove Jeffrey to school so early that he could have been the first person in the band room. But Jeffrey didn't go in. He couldn't. He knew what he'd see. Most of the kids would be there with trumpets or saxophones or flutes. Those instruments looked cool when you played them, Jeffrey thought. A clarinet looked like something that got stuck in your mouth and now you were waiting for a doctor or a plumber to come and remove it.

Finally he pushed the door open and went in to face the music. Mr. Rinaldi, the music teacher, was standing at the front of the room.

"Good morning," Mr. Rinaldi said coolly. "Name?"

"Jeffrey Becker," Jeffrey said.

"Oh, yes," Mr. Rinaldi answered. "You're the one who insisted on playing the clarinet, even though we already have more clarinets than we need." Jeffrey started to explain, but Mr. Rinaldi stopped him. "Never mind. Just take out your reeds and begin soaking them in your mouth. You do have reeds, don't you?"

"What are reeds?" Jeffrey asked.

"You don't have reeds, then," Mr. Rinaldi said with an impatient sigh. "So you'll have to watch this morning. Take a seat on the third level next to Simon Brandt. And try to pay attention, *in time* with the music."

Jeffrey climbed the platform to the third level of the band room. The seat Mr. Rinaldi had given him was right beside the drums. He looked at the drums longingly. Then he looked at the boy next to him. Simon Brandt was a fifth-grader. Jeffrey knew him from the playground. Everyone in school called him Simon Sez because he liked to tell people what to do.

"I'm Mr. Rinaldi's best clarinetist," Simon assured Jeffrey.

"Thanks. I feel a lot better already," said Jeffrey.

Simon gave Jeffrey a snooty look. "Just don't touch anything," he said. "Especially the drums."

"Let me have your attention, band," called Mr. Rinaldi. He was a short man with not very much hair, and he carried a cup of coffee with him at all times. "Take out your music. We'll start with 'Home on the Range.' Try to—"

But before Mr. Rinaldi could finish his sentence, he was interrupted by the boom of the bass drum.

Mr. Rinaldi looked up to where Jeffrey was sitting. "Jeffrey Becker, please leave the drums alone," he said.

"It wasn't me," Jeffrey said. "Must have

been thunder. Maybe it's going to rain." But he smiled to himself because he knew who it really was. Max was there!

"All right, let's play," Mr. Rinaldi said. "One, two, three, four . . ."

On the count of four, Max took off, playing. *Boom! Ba-ba-ba-boom!* He beat the drums in the most awesome rapid-fire drum solo Jeffrey had ever heard. Jeffrey couldn't believe how cool it sounded. He didn't know that Max could play the drums! Then, just as everyone in the room turned around to see who was playing, Max threw the drumsticks to Jeffrey.

"Catch, Daddy-o!" Max said with a laugh before he disappeared.

Jeffrey sat there with the clarinet in his lap and the drumsticks in his hands. To Mr. Rinaldi and everyone else in the band, it looked like Jeffrey had been playing the drums.

"That's it," Mr. Rinaldi yelled. "Jeffrey Becker, you're out of here!"

"I *told* you not to mess with those drums," Simon Sez said.

Jeffrey packed up his clarinet. But before he left the band room, he gave the cymbals a rim shot with the drumsticks. Then he walked out into the hall. Max was standing there with a drumstick between every finger and one between his teeth.

"Hey, Daddy-o! Did you groove on my sounds?"

"I dug them the most," Jeffrey replied, giving his friend a big smile.

"Like, I figured you wouldn't want to be stuck in a dragsville band sitting next to Simon Sez." Max drew a large square in the air with both index fingers.

"For sure," Jeffrey said. "Thanks for your help. I've really missed you, Max."

"Likewiseville," the ghost said. "You know, Daddy-o, I've been thinking. Like, maybe it wouldn't be so bad in the fourth grade. I'd get to hang out with all my old buddy-os, like you."

"All right!" Jeffrey said, cheering up. "But I don't think you can come to class unless you go to detention first. There are some things Miss Dotson doesn't forget, and you *did* make her pretty mad."

"I could swing with the detention scene," Max said. And to prove it, he floated up in the air and started swinging—without a swing.

"You mean you'll come to class?" Jeffrey asked hopefully.

"Maybe," said the ghost, starting to fade. "Toss you now and catch you later, Jeffrey."

The words *yes*, *definitely*, *positively*, or anything like them were not in Max's vocabulary.

"That's okay. You don't have to answer right away. No hurry," Jeffrey said, looking at thin air. "I'm still waiting for answers to stuff I asked you last year."

That night Jeffrey lay on his bed thinking about the fourth grade. So far, it had been nothing like the year before. So far, it stank—which was why Jeffrey really wanted Max to come back to class.

In the third grade Jeffrey had had a wonderful teacher named Mrs. Merrin who had treated him like a person instead of a kid. Now he had a teacher who couldn't remember the days of the week if they were tattooed on her arms.

In the third grade Jeffrey had had almost no homework. But in the fourth grade the work was really hard. He had tons of it every night.

But the biggest change was that in the third grade Jeffrey had met Max. And for most of the year Max was his own special friend. Now, all of Jeffrey's close friends knew about Max. It was cool, but it wasn't the same.

Worst of all, in the fourth grade, Max refused to go to school.

Everything was changing—and Jeffrey didn't like the changes one bit.

"Knock, knock." It was Jeffrey's father, poking his head into Jeffrey's room. "Family meeting in two minutes. Be there or be square," Mr. Becker said, smiling.

Jeffrey hurried downstairs to the living room. What now? he wondered.

"Hi, Mom and Dad," Jeffrey said. "What's up?"

Mr. Becker pointed to Jeffrey and then to a chair. Jeffrey sat down in the big flowered armchair.

"We have something to tell you," Jeffrey's mother began with a smile. "I'll bet you've been wondering why I enrolled you in so many after-school programs, haven't you?"

"Yeah," Jeffrey admitted. "It's a drag."

"The truth is, Jeffrey, we were trying to keep you busy. We thought maybe that way you wouldn't notice that you were getting less attention. And you wouldn't mind that things were changing around here," Mr. Becker explained. "But now we realize that wasn't the right thing to do. You've got to be part of the change."

Another change? Jeffrey winced. "What kind of change?" he asked.

"A good change," said Mr. Becker. "Your mother is going to have a baby."

"And you're going to have a baby brother or sister," said his mother. She was wearing her warmest smile for the occasion.

Jeffrey stared at his parents. "I am?" he said. He bent his legs and curled up on the big armchair he was sitting on.

After a long silence, Mr. Becker asked, "Well? What do you think?"

What *did* he think? Jeffrey wondered. A million things were going through his mind. But every time he tried to think of just one, he forgot them all. "I don't know," he said at last. "Are babies any fun?"

"You were," Mr. Becker told him.

"When is it coming?"

"This spring," said Mrs. Becker. "The baby will come with the flowers. Isn't that nice?"

"What if I don't like it?" Jeffrey asked.

"What if you do?" answered his father.

Jeffrey didn't know the answer to that question. Maybe he would like the baby, but it was too soon to tell.

Jeffrey started to think about all the things he might have to share when the baby came. His toys, his room, the TV . . .

And then suddenly Jeffrey had a brilliant idea. "I want to give the baby a present. Right now."

His parents smiled. They looked pleased.

"This is going to make me sad, but I really want to do it," Jeffrey said.

"I think you should trust your feelings, Jeffrey," said his mother. "And I'm sure we'll be proud of you."

"Are you sure?" he asked. "Even if it's something very precious to me?"

"Of course," his father replied, beaming proudly. "I knew you would handle this well. What is it? What do you want to give the baby?"

"Simple, Dad," Jeffrey said. "I'm going to give it my clarinet!"

Chapter Five

The next day was Saturday, and Jeffrey had a surprise visitor at noon. It was Melissa. He was surprised to see her because ever since the first day of school, when she lost her diary, Melissa had been acting weird. She hadn't even come over to Jeffrey's house all week.

"Hi, Jeffrey," said Melissa, standing in the doorway. "What are you doing to your room?"

Jeffrey looked up from his project. He was putting everything that used to be on the floor—stacks of comic books, dirty clothes, balls, bats, shoes, cassettes, toys—up on shelves at least three feet off the ground.

"It's called baby-proofing," Jeffrey answered, carrying an armful of football and baseball caps. He had a collection of caps from almost thirty different teams. "See this book? Ben gave it to me this morning. It's called *Getting Ready for Baby: Self-Defense for Brothers*. It says what the baby can't reach, the baby can't tear to pieces. So I'm putting everything of mine away."

"Baby? Brother?" Melissa's eyes practically turned into sparklers. "Jeffrey, are you going to be a big brother?" she squealed. Jeffrey nodded. "That's fantabulously terrific!"

Jeffrey was shocked. Melissa had never said anything like that before in her life. And he had never *ever* heard her squeal. "Melissa," he said, "what's wrong with you?"

"Wrong with *me*?" she asked.

"Yeah. You're acting like . . . well, not like yourself."

"And how am I acting, Jeffrey?" Melissa said challengingly. She put her hands on her hips, and her ponytail twitched as her eyes glared into Jeffrey's. Now *that* was more like Melissa.

"Well, for a moment there you were acting like a girl. I thought next you were going to tell me you were suddenly afraid of spiders."

Melissa rolled her eyes. "Don't be stupid, Jeffrey. But it's a baby we're talking about. They're so tiny and cute, and they look up at you and pull your nose, and they love you and you can dress them in cute clothes, and they smell so good."

"They do? That's not what Ben said. Ben said babies are a total drag," Jeffrey said. He grabbed the book Ben had loaned him and showed Melissa the table of contents. "Look at some of these chapters. 'Chapter One: Fighting back against drool. Chapter Two: Fifteen excuses for getting out of changing a baby that *always* work. Chapter Three: The Baby's Toys: How they compare to yours in real money.' "

Melissa grabbed the book out of Jeffrey's hands and threw it in the wastebasket. "That's garbage," she told him. "What's the matter with you? Do you want to be just like my brother Gary? Is that the kind of big brother you want to be?"

Jeffrey thought for a moment about the crummy way Gary treated Melissa. "Your brother does have a few faults," Jeffrey said. "Breathing is the biggest one."

"Right. And I wish he'd stop it," Melissa said. "Having a baby brother or sister is going to be great, Jeffrey. And I'll come over and help you do things."

"Like what?" Jeffrey asked.

"Well, I'll have to teach her to pitch because you certainly can't do it. I mean, your fastball has to take a bus to get to the plate. And your curveball doesn't curve, and—"

"Okay, I get the picture," Jeffrey said.

"So I'll teach her how to play baseball and to climb trees, and I'll take her camping and—"

"Hey, that's enough. It's *my* sister, you know."

"But you said babies are a drag," Melissa replied.

"Well, maybe. I don't know," said Jeffrey. "But I'll think about it."

"Okay." Melissa nodded.

"So, anyway, why did you come over?" Jeffrey asked.

"I was going to go somewhere and I was wondering if you wanted to come along."

"I might," said Jeffrey, sitting down on the floor in front of his bed. "Where are you going?"

"To Miss Dotson's house."

Jeffrey leaped to his feet so fast that Melissa stepped back in surprise. "No way," Jeffrey said. "Are you kidding? Weekends are the only time I don't have school or after-school or before-school. I am absolutely not going over to a teacher's house on a Saturday."

"Please, Jeffrey. I can't go alone."

"Why do you have to go at all?" Jeffrey asked.

"To get my diary. Miss Dotson has had it for two weeks and she won't give it back to me. I've tried every day after school to get it from her, but she's always busy with meetings or something else. So I'm going to get her where she lives, as they say—for real."

"Look, Melissa, give up on that diary. I'll lend you some money to buy a new one, okay?"

"No, Jeffrey. I've got to get that one back, and you've got to come with me."

"No, I don't," Jeffrey said quickly.

"Yes, you do," Melissa argued. "You're great at explaining things, Jeffrey. And Miss Dotson hates me. I'm the only kid she still calls by the wrong name. Do I look like a Gertrude?"

"If she already hates you, why are you worried if she reads your stupid diary? Did you write something about her?"

"I can't tell you," Melissa said. "It's a secret."

Jeffrey grabbed a football. "Come on, Melissa. Let's go play some ball or something."

Melissa stared at Jeffrey for a very long time without moving. Finally she said, "All right, I'm desperate. If I tell you what's in the diary, will you come with me?"

"Maybe. It depends on what it is."

"You've got to promise you won't tell anyone. You've got to put on your Red Sox cap that Carl Yastrzemski once wore and promise me you won't tell anyone."

"Okay. No problem," Jeffrey said. He sat down on his clean, empty desktop. "But can I tell Ben? He's my best friend."

"You can't tell *anyone*," said Melissa.

"Okay. No problem," Jeffrey repeated, nodding his head. "Can I tell Ricky? He's pretty good with secrets."

"Jeffrey! I'll *kill* you if you tell Ricky!"

"Well, it's no fun knowing a secret if you can't tell someone." He grinned. "Can I tell my baby brother or sister?"

"Jeffrey Becker! Stop teasing me. I'm going to tell you what's in my diary"—Melissa was almost gasping for air—"and I'll kill you if you tell a single soul!"

Jeffrey scratched his neck. "I'm waiting," he said.

Melissa looked away. "I wrote some things

in my diary about Ricky Reyes," she said quickly. Then she crossed her arms over her chest. "Because I like him."

"Sure, everybody likes Ricky. He's a cool guy," Jeffrey said.

Melissa shook her head and sighed. She looked at Jeffrey. "Don't you get it? I mean, I *like* him. I mean, not just as a friend, you know?"

It took a little while for Jeffrey to get from "not knowing" to "knowing" what Melissa meant. But finally he got there. "You mean you *like* Ricky Reyes?"

"Shh!" Melissa scolded. "I told you not to tell. Don't even tell *me*. Now do you see why I'd croak if Ricky found out?"

"Not exactly," Jeffrey said. "If you like him, why don't you want him to know that you like him?"

"Because that's how these things work. That's all. Now, will you *please* help me get my diary back? You promised."

"All right," Jeffrey grumbled. "Let's go."

The bike ride to Miss Dotson's neighborhood was a long one. But the warm Indian summer afternoon felt good. Not surprisingly, Miss Dotson lived in an old house. It was

made of red brick and faced a small park with tall, old trees.

Jeffrey and Melissa parked their bikes and climbed the concrete steps to the front door. A yellow cat with blue eyes meowed at them, but it was too drowsy to move from its sunny spot on the porch.

Jeffrey rang the bell and waited, then rang the bell again.

Finally Miss Dotson answered the door. She was wearing one of the dark blue dresses with small white polka dots that she wore at school. "Hello, Jeffrey and Gertrude," she said. "This is an interesting surprise. I didn't know you were coming, did I?"

"No," Melissa said.

"Neither did I," added Jeffrey.

"Well, come in," said the teacher, opening the door wider.

"Come in, Jeffrey and Gertrude," Melissa mumbled under her breath as the two kids stepped in.

"I was just about to have some tea and muffins," Miss Dotson said. They were standing in the hallway and Miss Dotson peeked into the living room. "No, not in here." Then she peeked into the den. "Where did I put that tea tray? Oh, well, follow me. We'll find it."

Melissa and Jeffrey followed Miss Dotson through the rooms of the house. Most of the furniture was made of old, dark wood. And in every room there were things that seemed to be out of place. Gardening tools in the library; rain boots in the dining room; construction paper, glitter, glue, and crayons in the bathroom. When Melissa saw the mess, her heart sank. "Forget it," she whispered to Jeffrey. "If it's here, I'll never find it."

Miss Dotson finally found her tray of tea and muffins in her study where she had been watching TV with the sound turned down. "Now, why did I tell you children to come over here?" she asked. "Your faces are pink. You've certainly been riding for a while."

"You didn't tell us to come over," Melissa said. She poked Jeffrey in the side. "Go on— ask her about the diary," she whispered.

Jeffrey shook his head and gave Melissa a "not yet" look. "We came over to tell you some good news," he said instead. "I'm going to have a baby brother or sister. I've never been anyone's brother before."

"Neither have I," said Miss Dotson. "That's

exciting. You're very lucky, Jeffrey. But I have a sister . . . oh, dear." Miss Dotson looked around the room. "I think I just lost her."

Losing a cup of tea was one thing, Jeffrey thought, but losing your sister was another!

Miss Dotson stood up and went from room to room once again. Finally she found a framed photograph on the screened porch. "Here she is. But this is when she was much younger," she said, pointing to a color photograph of a young red-haired girl with a ponytail. "This is my sister, Gertrude."

"Your sister's name is Gertrude?" Melissa asked.

Jeffrey could tell that Melissa was trying to tone down the surprise in her voice.

"Yes. She was very particular about always being called Gertrude. Never Trudy or Gertie. She lives in California, so we don't see each other very much. I really miss her."

Melissa looked at Jeffrey and smiled. Then she straightened her own red ponytail a little bit.

"You know, sometimes you call me Gertrude, Miss Dotson," Melissa said.

Miss Dotson looked at Melissa, then at the old photograph. "I do?" the teacher asked. "I'm sorry, dear."

"Oh, that's okay," Melissa said quickly. "I don't mind."

Jeffrey choked when Melissa said that, but she ignored him and went on. "Miss Dotson, could I ask you about my diary?" she said. "I really need it back."

"I don't understand," said Miss Dotson.

"You still have my diary," Melissa told her.

"No, no, no. I returned that to you days ago," said the teacher. "Are you sure you haven't misplaced it?"

"*Me?*" Melissa said. "I didn't misplace it. Miss Dotson, my diary is still in your desk drawer."

"No, it can't be. I know everything that's in there."

"Even the stuff that's multiplying?" asked Jeffrey under his breath.

"I know I gave it back to you because I

know that diaries are very important," Miss Dotson said. "Once Gertrude stole one of my diaries from under my pillow. I was probably about your age. Well, she read it and showed it to every one of her friends. And I was beside myself with anger and embarrassment."

Melissa was turning paler by the second.

"Diaries hold all of our secrets," the teacher went on. "That's why you've got to learn to hang on to them." And with that she got up and showed them to the door. "It was very nice of you to visit," she called out as she waved good-bye.

"Great of us," Melissa muttered as she swung her leg over her bike. She looked so miserable that for the first time Jeffrey felt really sorry for her. "Do you think I'll ever get my diary back?" she asked glumly.

"I don't know, but at least you tried," he answered, hoping he could cheer her up.

"Who cares about times at bat?" Melissa replied. "I wanted a home run."

Jeffrey sighed. "In that case, I think it's time to send in the designated hitter."

"Who's that?" Melissa asked.

"Who do you think?" Jeffrey answered with a grin. "Max!"

Chapter Six

Jeffrey spread the map out on his kitchen table so that he could go over the plan one more time. It was Monday morning, 0700 hours, half an hour before they hit their target. Jeffrey pointed at different locations on the map as he briefed the team. The team consisted of Jeffrey, Max, Ben, and Melissa.

"Okay, listen up. Here's the school, here's Miss Dotson's room, here's Miss Dotson's desk where the diary is, and here's the North Pole where Santa Claus lives," Jeffrey began.

"Hey, Daddy-o. What's Daddy-ho-ho-ho doing on your map?" asked Max.

"Because if he finds out we're breaking into a teacher's desk, he's going to be sending us yearly shipments of coal till we're fifteen," Jeffrey answered. "Now, here's my plan. As soon as Miss Dotson opens up her classroom, I'll come rushing in. I'll tell her that Melissa was sacked by a blitzing cornerback in the

parking lot. She won't know that's a football term, so she'll jump up and run to see if Melissa is okay. Then Max will sneak into the room and unlock the desk so that we can get the diary before Miss Dotson comes back."

"Daddy-o, is this plan for real?"

"Max, I know it'll work," Jeffrey said. "I saw it on a TV cartoon show last Saturday."

Melissa looked troubled. "Isn't there another way to get my diary?" she asked.

Jeffrey nodded. "I suppose we could use a hyperalloy metric laser probe," he said.

"Well, that sounds okay to me," Melissa said.

Jeffrey shook his head. "There's only one problem. It hasn't been invented yet. I just made it up."

Ben looked thoughtful. "I could work on it," he offered.

"Too late, Daddy-os. Like, I made one of those a couple weeks ago," Max said, taking three sweet rolls from a box on the counter. "But too badsville. I loaned it to a cat and he didn't give it back."

"Sure, Max," Jeffrey said. "Well, Melissa, if you want your diary back, it looks like it's my plan or zip. And, Max, you'd better leave

62

some sweet rolls for my dad. He bought them especially for himself."

The ghost hid the empty sweet roll package behind his back and cleared his throat. "Jeffrey, haven't you told your old man that cereal is, like, a lot groovier for his health?"

By seven-thirty, which Jeffrey called 0730 hours, the team was in place outside the school. The plan was for Melissa and Ben to stay outside. Jeffrey stood on the school stairs, waiting for Miss Dotson, who was always the first teacher to arrive.

As soon as she opened her classroom and turned on the lights, Jeffrey went charging in to see her.

"Miss Dotson! Miss Dotson! Melissa's just been sacked by a blitzing cornerback in the parking lot!" he shouted.

The teacher, who was writing on the chalkboard, turned around, looking concerned. "Well, tell her to fake an off-tackle run and set up a screen pass," she told him. "That'll fix their wagons."

Jeffrey's wagon got fixed at that moment, too. Much to his surprise, Miss Dotson was an expert on football plays. "I'll tell her later," Jeffrey said. "Her team is winning, anyway."

Jeffrey had to think quickly. There had to be another way to get the teacher out of the classroom—and fast before the other kids arrived for school. He decided to try the Max attack.

"Miss Dotson, did you really see a ghost in this room?" he asked.

"You know I did, don't you, Jeffrey?" said the teacher. "I had a strange feeling for many years that there was a ghost in this school. I never said anything to anyone, and I never saw him. But I told myself, this ghost needs a friend. That's what he's looking for."

"I know where he lives," Jeffrey said.

"I thought so," Miss Dotson replied.

"He lives in a desk in Mrs. Merrin's room," Jeffrey said, watching a sparkle come into his teacher's eyes.

"A third-grade class?"

"He's always been a third-grader," Jeffrey explained.

"I'll have a talk with him. It's time he graduated," Miss Dotson said briskly. Then she locked her desk and went down the hall to Mrs. Merrin's third-grade class.

As soon as Miss Dotson was gone, Max

floated into the room. "Cool move, Daddy-o, but what's this about graduationsville?"

"Max, let's just get the diary and worry about that later," Jeffrey urged. "She won't be gone for long."

"Daddy-o, it doesn't take long to do what must be done," said the ghost. He floated over to the teacher's desk. "Dig this. Nothing up my sleeve." As he said it, Max held out his right arm and made his hand disappear and reappear a couple of times. "Then we groove on the ever-so-grooveable magic words: Through the numbers and past the sums, look out, diary, here Max comes."

Then the ghost stretched out his hand—and pushed it right *through* the wooden desk drawer! Jeffrey held his breath while Max pushed until his arm was all the way inside the desk. Then he started to feel around inside. "Daddy-o, I found something," Max said. "Like, I think I've got the diary—oh, no."

"Max, what happened? Did you lose it?"

"It's not the diary. I just squashed an old peanut-butter-and-jelly sandwich—complete yucksville."

"What about the diary, Max?"

"No sale, Jeffrey," Max said. "I don't think it's in there."

"My goodness," said a voice from in front of them. Jeffrey looked up and saw Miss Dotson standing there.

Jeffrey froze. He hadn't heard her come into the room.

"I just searched every desk in Mrs. Merrin's room looking for the ghost. I didn't think to search mine," she said. "What are you two up to?"

"Miss Dotson, I can explain this," Jeffrey said.

"No, Miss Dotson, *I* can explain this," said Melissa, who was standing in the doorway behind the teacher.

"Well, Max? Can you explain this, too?" the teacher asked the ghost.

"Sure, teacher-o. I invented explanations," Max said, pulling his arm out of the teacher's desk.

"I'll bet you did," Miss Dotson replied.

"Miss Dotson, don't blame Jeffrey. He did it because of me," Melissa admitted. "I told him how much I wanted my diary back. And he and Max said they'd get it for me."

"But, Melissa, I've told you a hundred times that I gave it back to you," Miss Dotson said.

"But you didn't, Miss Dotson. And it's driving me nuts."

Miss Dotson's voice remained calm. "Dear, of course I gave it to you. Last Tuesday—it was after school, and you weren't here, so I put it in your locker. It was open at the time."

"You did? You never told me. And I haven't seen it there," Melissa said.

"Well, I put it right in locker 231."

Melissa's eyes rolled in her head.

"What's wrong?" Jeffrey asked.

"Oh, nothing," Melissa said. "Miss Dotson put my diary in locker 231, but my locker number happens to be 321."

Miss Dotson checked a list in one of her notebooks. "You're right on the money with that, Melissa. I guess I made a mistake."

"Hey, dig this. We'll just talk to the cat with locker 231 and zip-zop, boom-bang, the diary will be back in Melissa's hands in no time," Max suggested.

"Good idea. Let's see," Miss Dotson said, referring to her list again. "Okay, that will be Ricky Reyes."

"Oh, no! I don't believe it," Melissa

moaned. She wrapped her long ponytail around her head like a mummy. "Max?" she asked. "What does it feel like to be a ghost? Because, as of right now, I'm dead."

Jeffrey and Max followed Melissa as she ran out into the hall and tried to open Ricky Reyes's locker. It was locked. A few moments later, Ricky came walking down the hall. He was wearing dark sunglasses and a fluorescent purple jacket. "Hey, Jeffrey. Hey, Melissa. Hey, Max. Long time no see," Ricky said. He started to walk into the classroom.

"Hey, aren't you going to put your jacket in your locker?" Jeffrey asked.

Ricky shrugged. "Uh-uh."

"Jeffrey, do something—quick!" Melissa said, hiding her face in her hands.

"Uh, Ricky," Jeffrey said, "don't tell me you're not going to open your locker. What if yours is the winner?"

"The what?" Ricky asked.

"One of the fourth-grade lockers has a red question mark painted inside it. If it's yours, you win a prize."

"Forget it," Ricky said. "Contests are for suckers."

Melissa took a deep breath and let it out as

she spoke. "Uh, Ricky, let me put it another way. Did you happen to find something in your locker?"

"Like what?" Ricky asked.

"Oh, nothing really," said Melissa. "You know, it's just kind of a silly mistake and everything. But maybe you found something that looked like a notebook or a diary or something. And, I mean, it would be lying there just sort of saying 'Read me, read me.' But you wouldn't do that, would you?"

"Melissa, you've been hanging around Miss Dotson too long," Ricky said. "I don't know what you're talking about."

Melissa put her hands on her hips and came right up close to Ricky, backing him against the wall. "Ricky Reyes, did you find my diary in your locker and did you read it?"

"Your diary? How'd your diary get into my locker?"

"Here's a hinterino," said Max. "It's, like, someone who calls you Rocky Reyes when you go to class."

Ricky laughed. "Miss Dotson put *your* diary in *my* locker? I'll bet that really bummed you out."

70

"Yeah, it did. So did you read it or didn't you?" Melissa said, nearly bursting.

"Read it? I haven't even opened my locker since the first day of school. I've got a strict policy. I put my books in there on day one and I don't look at them again until the end of the year when we turn them in."

"You mean you haven't opened your locker?" Melissa said. She laughed a strange laugh, but she was starting to sound happy. "My diary has been safe all the time?"

"Hey, I don't even remember the combination," Ricky said.

"No problemsville," the ghost said quickly. "Yours truly to the rescue once again."

While Melissa was laughing, Max slipped *through* the door of Ricky's locker. And in another minute he was laughing, too.

"Max, what's so funny?" Jeffrey asked.

"Be out in sixty ticks, cats," Max said, laughing again.

"Max, what are you doing?" Melissa asked.

"Reading!" the ghost said with a burst of laughter.

"Max! Get out of there, you creep!" Melissa shouted, pounding on the door to the locker.

Of course, neither Max nor Jeffrey were laughing after school that day. They were sitting in Miss Dotson's classroom, alone. They both had detention for breaking into Miss Dotson's desk. Miss Dotson was in the office picking up her mail.

"Like old timesville, Daddy-o," said the ghost, sitting in midair. "Hey, remember your first detention when I squirted you with your own squirt gun?"

Jeffrey remembered. That was the first time he met Max, a year ago.

Splat! Right then Max squirted Jeffrey with a squirt gun he had hidden under his shirt. "Old timesville," said the ghost again.

Jeffrey wiped his face on his shirt and grinned. Then he got serious for a minute. "Max, can I ask you something?"

"Shoot," said the ghost.

"Did you ever have any brothers or sisters?" Jeffrey asked.

The ghost shook his head. "My old man always used to tell me I was more than any two parents could handle," Max said. "He dug me the most. Why do you ask?"

"Because I'm going to be a brother," Jeffrey said.

"Like, that's an utter gas, Daddy-o!"

"How would you know? You never were a brother."

"Jeffrey, like, I never was a banana split, either, but I know everything there is to know about them. Brothers and sisters are the coolest. Like, when they're older, you can tease them and borrow all their best toys and, like, say you didn't. And half the time your folks believe you."

"But I'm talking about a little baby, Max."

"Oh," the ghost said thoughtfully. "Like, it's different when they're baby-os. You've got to be cool with them so they know what's hip. You can forget worrysville, Daddy-o. Yours truly will be with you every step of the way. With Max in charge, this is going to be one very cool baby!"

Just then Miss Dotson walked into the classroom. "What are you two doing in here?" she asked pleasantly.

"We have a detention," Jeffrey said. "Remember?"

"Well," said the teacher, "I remember that you already stayed after school yesterday."

"Did we?" asked Jeffrey.

"Like, probably," Max said quickly.

"So go home. I'm tired of seeing you after school every day," Miss Dotson said.

Jeffrey and Max were halfway out the door when the teacher said, "Wait a minute. Before you go, I have something for you."

She motioned them to come back to her desk with a tilt of her head. "Take a look at this," she said. "It's the class seating chart. And there's an empty seat right in front of Becky Dancer."

"Becky Singer," Jeffrey corrected her.

"I thought so," said the teacher. "Well, anyway, I want to put a name on the chart." She picked up a pen and wrote MAX in the empty space. "What do you think?"

Max looked at his name on the paper for a moment. Then he looked around the classroom and at Jeffrey. Finally he smiled. "Okay," he said. "Like, through the numbers and past the sums, look out fourth grade, here Max comes!"

Here's a peek at Jeffrey's next adventure with Max, the fourth-grade ghost:

BASEBALL CARD FEVER

Max ran a hand through his slicked-back hair. "I promised and I delivered, Daddy-o. I gave you back your baseball cards."

"No, you didn't," Jeffrey argued. "I looked inside my desk. They weren't in there."

"That's because I laid them *on* your desk," answered the ghost.

Jeffrey started walking in circles. "*On* my desk?! I said put them *in* my desk!"

"On . . . in . . . like, what's the big dif, Daddy-o? I only blew it by one letter."

"Wait a minute, Jeffrey. The cards weren't on your desk when you got to class, right?" Melissa said.

Jeffrey nodded.

"So, what happened to them?" asked Ben.

There was only one answer, but it was too awful to be true. "Someone took them," Jeffrey said.

Max's eyes widened. "You mean, thievesville?"

ABOUT THE AUTHORS

Bill and Megan Stine have written many books and stories for young readers including several in these series: *The Three Investigators*; *Wizards, Warriors, and You*; and *Find Your Fate: Indiana Jones*. They live in Atlanta, Georgia, with their son, Cody.